The Splendid POOL

Written by
Laura Appleton-Smith

Illustrated by
Preston Neel

Laura Appleton-Smith was born and raised in Vermont and holds a degree in English from Middlebury College. Laura is a primary school teacher who has combined her talents in creative writing and her experience in early childhood education to create *Books to Remember*. Laura lives in New Hampshire with her husband, Terry.

Preston Neel was born in Macon, Georgia. Greatly inspired by Dr. Seuss, he decided to become an artist at the age of four. Preston's advanced art studies took place at the Academy of Art College San Francisco. Now Preston pursues his career in art with the hope of being an inspiration himself, particularly to children who want to explore their endless bounds.

A Book to Remember™
Published by Flyleaf Publishing

For orders or information, contact us at **(800) 449-7006**.
Please visit our website at **www.flyleafpublishing.com**

Eighth Edition 2/20
Library of Congress Control Number: 2009937028
ISBN-13: 978-1-60541-021-0
Printed and bound in the USA at Worzalla Publishing, Stevens Point, WI

Thanks to Aesop for these classic fables.

LAS

—

Thanks to Kathie and Peter for being such good sports.

PN

Chapter 1

Luke and June spent all their wedded days living in a one-room log cabin.

The cute cabin had a grass roof that bloomed in the spring, and a stoop with stools to sit upon in the afternoon.

The cabin sat on a plot of land
at the bottom of a looming rock cliff.

Next to the cliff was a pool of water.
The pool was filled by a river that spewed,
as if by magic, from a crack
in the looming rocks.

Luke and June planted crops of carrots.
Day after day they tended their crops
and watered them from the pool.

The carrots grew and grew. In fact, June and Luke grew
the biggest and best carrots in all of the land.

Chapter 2

One spring day, as June and Luke tended their crops, a goose and gander flew past.

The geese looped back over the blooming cabin roof and past the rock cliff.

Then they swooped down and landed on the pool.

8

The goose and gander began constructing a nest.

As June and Luke sat on their stoop that afternoon,
they were filled with gladness.

They were not rich with silver or jewels,
but there was richness and a bit of magic
in living next to a splendid pool of water.

Chapter 3

The next day was cool and the wind was gusting. As Luke filled his bucket, the wind lifted his hat up and blew it into the pool.

The hat spooked the goose and she flew from her nest. It was then that Luke spotted a glint...

Luke crept up to the nest.
In it was a silver egg twinkling in the sun.

Luke could not help himself.
He lifted up the egg in his hands.
It was solid silver—as solid as a rock.

June was on the stoop with her broom
when she spotted Luke running at her.
He was hooting and hollering as he ran.
"We are rich! We are rich!" he yelled.

June was confused. Then she spotted the silver egg in Luke's hands.

Chapter 4

"Put on your boots. Bring this egg to the bank. Run as fast as you can!" Luke begged June. "I cannot go myself. I have a job to do."

June's mood filled with gloom. Why was she so sad if she was so rich?

As June trekked to the bank, Luke got out his tools.

He constructed a coop for the goose and put it on top of her and her nest.

When June got back from the bank she was met by a sad song.

Next to the pool she spotted the coop with the goose in it.

Next to the coop was the gander, crooning a sad tune.

Chapter 5

Luke spent day after day with the goose,
begging her for a second silver egg.

June tended the carrots herself,
but there was too much to do.

The carrots got less and less water
and wilted.

The mood on the plot of land that spring was sad.

The goose just slept in the coop.

The gander roosted on the roof that no longer bloomed.

Even the river that spewed from the rocks was just a trickle.

Then one day, Luke put on his boots. He kissed June, and left.

When Luke got back that afternoon, he lifted the coop off of the nest. He put the silver egg back under the goose. "I am a fool," Luke said. Then he got his bucket and went off to water the wilting carrot crop.

Chapter 6

Spring bloomed into summer, and then summer cooled to fall.

Under the harvest moon, Luke and June sat on their stoop.
As they sipped cups of carrot stew, they were filled with gladness.

The river spewed from the rocks.
The goose and gander swam in the pool with their brood of goslings.
The silver egg sat in the nest, glinting under the moon.

When the geese flew off that winter,
they left the silver egg for Luke and June.

The egg was not put in the bank.
It sat on the sill in the one-room log cabin,
where it glinted in the winter sun.

Chapter 7

When winter melted into spring, the goose and gander flew back. They looped over the blooming grass roof, past the rock cliff, and landed on the splendid pool.

There never was a second silver egg.

But for Luke and June,
there was richness and magic
living on a plot of land
next to a splendid pool of water.

Prerequisite Skills

Single consonants and short vowels
Final double consonants **ff**, **gg**, **ll**, **nn**, **ss**, **tt**, **zz**
Consonant /k/ **ck**
Consonant /j/ **g**, **dge**
Consonant /s/ **c**
/ng/ **n[k]**
Consonant digraphs /ng/ **ng**, /th/ **th**, /hw/ **wh**
Consonant digraphs /ch/ **ch**, **tch**, /sh/ **sh**, /f/ **ph**
Schwa /ə/ **a**, **e**, **i**, **o**, **u**
Long /ā/ **a_e**
Long /ē/ **e_e**, **ee**, **y**
Long /ī/ **i_e**, **igh**
Long /ō/ **o_e**
Long /ū/, /o͞o/ **u_e**
r-Controlled /ar/ **ar**
r-Controlled /or/ **or**
r-Controlled /ûr/ **er**, **ir**, **ur**, **ear**, **or**, **[w]or**
/ô/ **al**, **all**
/ul/ **le**
/d/ or /t/ **–ed**

Target Letter-Sound Correspondence

Long /o͞o/ sound spelled **oo**

afternoon	looming
bloomed	looped
blooming	mood
boots	moon
brood	pool
broom	roof
cool	room
cooled	roosted
coop	spooked
crooning	stools
fool	stoop
gloom	swooped
goose	too
hooting	tools

Target Letter-Sound Correspondence

Long /o͞o/ and long /ū/ sounds spelled **ew**

blew	jewels
flew	spewed
grew	stew

Target Letter-Sound Correspondence

Long /o͞o/ and long /ū/ sounds spelled **u_e**

confused	Luke
cute	Luke's
June	tune
June's	

High-Frequency Puzzle Words

are	one
began	out
by	over
could	put
day	said
days	she
do	so
down	their
even	there
from	they
go	to
have	was
he	we
into	were
living	where
myself	why
no	you
of	your

Decodable Words

1	can	glinting	left	rocks	then
2	cannot	goslings	less	run	this
3	carrot	got	lifted	running	top
4	carrots	grass	log	sad	trekked
5	chapter	gusting	longer	sat	trickle
a	cliff	had	magic	second	twinkling
after	constructed	hands	melted	sill	under
all	constructing	harvest	met	silver	up
am	crack	hat	much	sipped	upon
and	crept	help	nest	sit	water
as	crop	her	never	slept	watered
at	crops	herself	next	solid	wedded
back	cups	himself	not	song	went
bank	egg	his	off	spent	when
begged	fact	hollering	on	splendid	wilted
begging	fall	I	or	spotted	wilting
best	fast	if	past	spring	wind
biggest	filled	in	planted	summer	winter
bit	for	It	plot	sun	with
bottom	gander	job	ran	swam	yelled
bring	geese	just	rich	tended	
bucket	gladness	kissed	richness	that	
but	glint	land	river	the	
cabin	glinted	landed	rock	them	